This LADYBIRD TALE
belongs to

....

Beauty
and the Beast

Retold by Vera Southgate M.A., B.COM
with illustrations by Yunhee Park

LADYBIRD TALES

ONCE UPON A TIME, in a town far away, there lived a rich merchant who had three pretty daughters.

The youngest daughter was the prettiest of the three and she was called Beauty. She was as good and kind as she was lovely. Her elder sisters, although they too were pretty, were neither kind nor good. They were selfish and proud.

One day their father came home looking very grave. When his daughters asked him what was the matter, he replied, "Alas, I am no longer rich. I have lost my fortune. We must all leave this beautiful house and go to live in a cottage in the country."

The elder sisters were very angry when they learned this news.

"What shall we do with ourselves all day in the country?" they asked.

Beauty said, "How nice it will be to live in the country among the woods and fields and flowers."

So their father found a little cottage with a large garden in the country, and they all went to live there.

The father worked hard in the garden and, by selling his fruit and vegetables, made enough money to live comfortably.

One day, the father gathered his three daughters together and told them that he had to go to a distant town, on business. He might not return until the next day.

"Is there any little gift which I might bring home for you?" he asked each of his daughters in turn.

"Diamonds for me," said the eldest daughter.

"Pearls for me," said the second daughter.

"Please, Father, a bunch of white roses for me," said Beauty.

Then their father rode away on horseback and Beauty waved to him from the doorstep.

When the merchant had finished his business he set off for home. Before long it grew dark and he lost his way. He found himself in a dense wood and could find no way out.

Then, at last, he saw a light in the distance and he rode towards it. However, as he drew nearer to the light, he found that the trees formed a wide avenue. He rode up the avenue and, to his surprise, arrived at the entrance to a palace.

The door of the palace stood open, but there was no one in sight so the merchant walked in. He went into a room on the right of the hall, where a fire blazed in the hearth. There he found a table set with supper for one.

The merchant was hungry and decided that he would first take his horse to the stable. Then he would return and, if there was still no one in the room, he would have a good meal.

When he returned from the stable, the room was still empty so he sat down and enjoyed the supper.

After supper, Beauty's father felt sleepy and, crossing the hall, he found a bedroom all ready for use. He went to bed and slept soundly until the next morning.

When he awoke, his own clothes were nowhere to be seen but a new, embroidered suit lay on the chair, in their place. He dressed himself in the new clothes and then he set off for the stables, to see to his horse.

On the way to the stables, the merchant passed a beautiful rose garden. The sight of a white rose bush reminded him of Beauty's wish and he left the path to gather a bunch of the roses.

He had only picked one rose when he heard a terrible sound behind him. Turning round he saw a big beast.

The big beast said, in a big voice, "You ungrateful man! Whose bed did you sleep in? Whose food have you eaten? And whose clothes are you wearing? Mine, mine, mine! And you repay my kindness by stealing my roses. You shall die!"

The big beast looked so fierce that the poor man was terrified.

"Please do not kill me," he begged.

"Your life will be spared on one condition," replied the beast. "You must come back here in a month's time, bringing with you whatever shall first meet you on your return home."

Beauty's father could not do other than agree to this.

As the merchant rode away from the palace, he thought about the promise he had given to the beast.

Then he remembered how Beauty had stood waving to him as he left home. An awful thought struck him. "What if it is Beauty who first greets me on my return?"

Meanwhile, Beauty waited at the window of her room, watching for her dear father to return. When she saw a figure on horseback appear in the distance, she skipped down the garden path.

Yes, it was her dear father returning home, but Beauty could not think what was wrong with him. He looked so tired and sad.

"Father, are you not glad to see me?" asked Beauty.

"Glad? Oh, my little Beauty," cried the poor merchant.

When they reached the cottage, the merchant told his daughter of his promise to the beast. "But you shall not return with me, Beauty, whatever happens," he said.

Beauty, however, insisted that once a promise was made, it should be kept. Finally her father agreed that, at the end of the month, he would take her to the beast.

The end of the month came all too quickly and the merchant and his beloved daughter set off through the woods.

Towards nightfall, Beauty and her father arrived at the palace in the wood. They walked in and found a dainty supper for two was laid out on the table.

As they sat at the table, a terrible sound was heard at the door. It was the beast.

The beast turned to Beauty's father and asked, "Is this the daughter for whom you gathered the white roses?"

"Yes," said the merchant.

"She need not be sorry," said the beast, "for everything in the palace is for her use. Her room is ready now. Goodnight."

When Beauty reached her room, she found it more beautiful than any she had ever seen. Quite tired out, she was soon fast asleep.

In the morning, Beauty and her father had breakfast together. Then they said goodbye. When her father had ridden out of sight, Beauty went to her room. On one wall hung a mirror and beneath it, in letters of gold, was written:

"Little Beauty, dry your eyes,
Needless are those tears and sighs;
Gazing in this looking-glass,
What you wish shall come to pass."

These lines comforted Beauty, for she thought that if she were very unhappy she could wish herself at home again.

The days which followed seemed long to Beauty. Yet the beast had left many things for her amusement.

Sometimes she read and sometimes she painted. Some days she played outside in the gardens and on other days she gathered the beautiful flowers.

Each evening, at supper-time, the same sound was heard at the door and a big voice asked, "May I come in?" And each evening Beauty, trembling, answered, "Yes, Beast." Then they talked together.

Although the beast's body and voice terrified Beauty, his words were so kind that she soon grew less afraid of him.

"Am I very ugly, Beauty?" the beast asked one evening.

"Yes, Beast."

"And very stupid?"

"No, not stupid, Beast."

"Could you love me, Beauty?"

"Yes, I do love you, Beast, for you are so kind."

"Then will you marry me, Beauty?"

"Oh! No, no, Beast."

The beast seemed so unhappy that Beauty felt very miserable. "But I could not marry a beast," she said to herself.

The next morning Beauty looked into her mirror. "I wish I could know how my dear father is," she said. Then, as she gazed into the looking-glass, she saw a sad picture. Her father lay ill in bed and no one was looking after him. Beauty cried all day to think of his pain and his loneliness.

When the beast paid his usual visit in the evening, he saw how sad Beauty looked.

"What is the matter, Beauty?" he asked. She then told him why she was so unhappy and she begged him to let her go home.

"It will break my heart if you go, Beauty," said the beast.

"Yet I cannot bear to see you weep," went on the beast. "You shall go home tomorrow."

"Thank you, Beast," said Beauty, "but I will not break your heart. I shall come back within a week."

The beast looked very doubtful, for he was afraid he was going to lose Beauty for ever.

"Take this ring," he said sadly, "and if you should wish to come back, lay it on your table before you go to bed at night. And now, goodbye, my Beauty."

That night Beauty looked in the mirror and wished that next morning she might wake up in her father's cottage.

Beauty's wish came true, for next morning she found herself at home again.

From the very moment he saw her, Beauty's father began to get better. She could hardly believe it when she found a week had passed. But, although her father was much improved, Beauty did not feel that he was yet well enough to be left with her unkind sisters.

"I shall stay for one more week," said Beauty, and her father smiled happily at this news.

However, only a day or two had passed when Beauty had a dream. She dreamt that the beast was lying on the grass, near the white rose bush in the palace garden. He was saying "Oh! Beauty, Beauty, you said you would come back. I shall die without you."

This dream wakened Beauty and she could not bear to think of the poor beast. She jumped out of bed and laid the magic ring on her table. Then she fell asleep again.

When she woke in the morning, she was in her own room in the beast's palace.

Beauty knew that the beast never came to see her until the evening and yet the day seemed as if it would never end. At last supper-time came, but the beast did not arrive.

Poor Beauty felt miserable. At last a sudden thought struck her. What if her dream was true? What if the beast was lying on the grass near the rose bush?

Beauty ran out into the darkness of the palace garden and made her way towards the white rose bush. There, lying on the wet grass beneath the rose bush, she found the beast. She knelt down beside him on the grass and put her hand on his head. At her touch the beast opened his eyes.

"I cannot live without you, Beauty," he whispered, "so I am starving myself to death. Now that I have seen your face again, I shall die content."

"Oh, dear Beast, I cannot bear it if you die," said Beauty. "Please live and I will marry you. I love you, I really do. You have such a kind heart."

When Beauty had spoken these words, she hid her face in her hands and cried and cried. When she looked up, the beast was gone and a handsome prince stood by her side. He thanked her for freeing him.

"What do you mean?" asked Beauty, surprised. "Oh! I want my Beast, my dear Beast and nobody else!"

Then the prince explained. "A wicked fairy enchanted me and said I must be a beast and seem stupid and ugly," he told her. "Only a beautiful lady who was willing to marry me could break the spell. You are the beautiful lady, Beauty," went on the prince. Then the prince kissed Beauty and led her towards the palace. Soon a good fairy appeared, bringing with her Beauty's father.

Beauty married the prince and, with her dear father near her, lived happily ever after.

A History of Beauty and the Beast

The most well-known version of *Beauty and the Beast* was written by Madame Leprince de Beaumont in 1757. The tale was published in her *Magasin des enfants* and has since gone on to inspire books and films, including Walt Disney's much-loved 1991 animated film.

Leprince de Beaumont's plot features many of the same elements we expect to find in the tale today. There is a merchant with a beautiful daughter, a beast living a solitary life in a large palace and two jealous, self-centred sisters. The tale portrays a kind, beautiful young woman who accepts and loves another, regardless of the beast's appearance.

It further warns readers, through the characters of Beauty's sisters, against personal vanity and sisterly jealousy.

Ladybird's 1967 retelling, written by Vera Southgate is a classic of its time and has helped to bring the story to a new generation.

Collect more fantastic
LADYBIRD 🐞 TALES

Little Red
Riding Hood

9781409311126

Goldilocks
and the
Three Bears

9781409311119

Cinderella

9781409311072

Jack
and the
Beanstalk

9781409311102

The
Gingerbread
Man

9781409311096

The Three
Little Pigs

9781409311089

The Three Billy
Goats Gruff

9781409311065

Hansel
and
Gretel

9781409311133

Puss in Boots

9781409311225

Rapunzel

9781409311195

Rumpelstiltskin

9781409311164

The Elves and the
Shoemaker

9781409311188

Snow White and the Seven Dwarfs
9781409311171

The Enormous Turnip
9781409311218

The Magic Porridge Pot
9781409311201

Sleeping Beauty
9781409311157

The Princess and the Frog
9780718192556

Dick Whittington
9780718192532

The Big Pancake
9780718192549

Beauty and the Beast
9780241312254

Endpapers taken from series 606d,
first published in 1964

LADYBIRD BOOKS

UK | USA | Canada | Ireland | Australia
India | New Zealand | South Africa

Ladybird Books is part of the Penguin Random House group of companies
whose addresses can be found at global.penguinrandomhouse.com.

www.penguin.co.uk   www.puffin.co.uk   www.ladybird.co.uk

First published 2013. This edition 2017
001

Printed in Slovakia

A CIP catalogue record for this book is available from the British Library

ISBN: 978–0–241–31225–4

All correspondence to:
Ladybird Books
Penguin Random House Children's
80 Strand, London WC2R 0RL